Blake the Brave

WRITTEN BY JENNY PHILLIPS

ILLUSTRATED BY EKATERINA KOLESNIKOVA

- To Ben, a brave boy -

CHAPTER 1

Blake lived in a far-off land. His home was on top of a cliff.

Blake loved his home. He liked to read books by the arch.

He liked to look at the moss
on the stone walls.

He liked to play chess with his dad.

He liked to walk in the big
maze by the garden.

It seemed that Blake could not be scared. He held big crabs.

He rode his horse fast up slopes on the shore.

He swung on long green vines

that hung from tall trees.

He did not get scared if his
room was dark. If the wind

made loud sounds or an owl
hooted, he did not care.

It did not scare Blake to go
deep into caves with his dad.

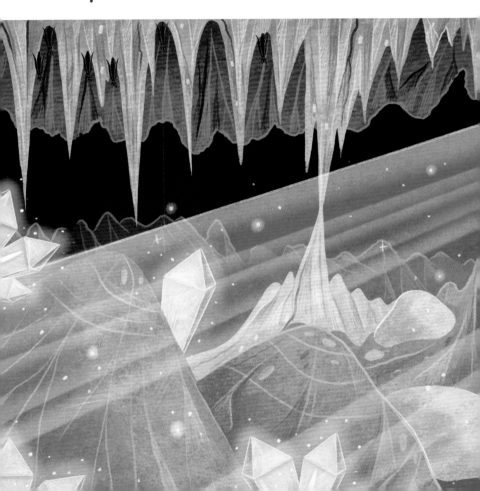

He was fine to go down on long ropes. It was no problem!

There was one thing that scared Blake—rats! He could not stand them.

Blake was so scared of rats that Blake's dad got a cat. The cat scared off a lot of the rats.

CHAPTER 2

Blake loved his mom. She did
so much for him. She took him

to the river. She hummed songs to him. She helped him look for frogs and nests. Blake and his mom had a lot of fun.

Blake's mom had a big chest.
She put her best things in it,

such as rings, soft silk cloth, and a vase.

One day Blake was setting up a game of chess.

Blake and his dad were going to play at lunchtime.

Just then, Blake spotted a rat.
It was running to the chest.

The rat was going to take
Mom's soft silk cloth!

The cat was not there to scare the rat.

"I must be brave," said Blake.
"I must scare the rat."

Blake yelled and ran at the rat.

Zip! Dash! The rat ran out of the home.

CHAPTER 3

Blake was so glad that he had saved the cloth for his mom.

His mom was so glad, too. "You are Blake the Brave," she said. "Good job!"

As a man Blake the Brave was kind. He helped those in need.

He spent his time doing good
things.

Blake the Brave had two girls,
and he helped them to be brave,

too—riding up steep hills, going into caves, and doing good things.

MORE GOLD TALES FROM THE GOOD AND THE BEAUTIFUL LIBRARY

Jane and the King

By Jenny Phillips

Jack and the Lost Maze

By Jenny Phillips

LOOK FOR THESE SILVER TALES FROM THE GOOD AND THE BEAUTIFUL LIBRARY

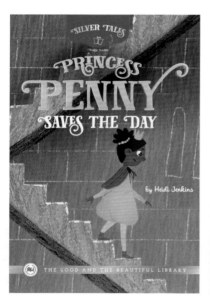

Princess Penny Saves the Day
By Heidi Jenkins

Peter the Persnickety
By Breckyn Wood